For Tom, David and Peter M.W.

For Amy and Sandy B.F.

First published 1996 by Walker Books Ltd
87 Vauxhall Walk, London SE11 5HJ

This edition published 2005

2 4 6 8 10 9 7 5 3

This book has been typeset in Monotype Columbus

Printed in China

British Library Cataloguing in Publication Data:
a catalogue record for this book
is available from the British Library

ISBN 1-84428-058-6 (hb)
ISBN 1-84428-494-8 (pb)

www.walkerbooks.co.uk

You and Me, Little Bear

Martin Waddell

illustrated by Barbara Firth

WALKER BOOKS

AND SUBSIDIARIES

LONDON • BOSTON • SYDNEY • AUCKLAND

Once there were two bears,
Big Bear and Little Bear.

Big Bear is the big bear

and Little Bear is the little bear.

Little Bear wanted to play, but

Big Bear had things to do.

"I want to play!" Little Bear said.

"I've got to get wood for the fire," said Big Bear.

"I'll get some too," Little Bear said.

"You and me, Little Bear," said Big Bear.

"We'll fetch the wood in together!"

"What shall we do now?" Little Bear asked.

"I'm going for water," said Big Bear.

"Can I come too?" Little Bear asked.

"You and me, Little Bear," said Big Bear.

"We'll go for the water together."

"Now we can play," Little Bear said.

"I've still got to tidy our cave," said Big Bear.

"Well … I'll tidy too!" Little Bear said.

"You and me," said Big Bear. "You tidy your things, Little Bear. I'll look after the rest."

"I've tidied my things, Big Bear!"

Little Bear said.

"That's good, Little Bear," said Big Bear.

"But I'm not finished yet."

"I want you to play!" Little Bear said.

"You'll have to play by yourself, Little Bear,"
said Big Bear. "I've still got plenty to do!"

Little Bear went to play by

himself, while Big Bear

got on with the work.

Little Bear played

bear-jump.

Little Bear

played

bear-slide.

Little Bear played
bear-swing.

Little Bear played
bear-tricks-with-bear-sticks.

Little Bear played bear-stand-on-his-head

and Big Bear came out to sit on his rock.

Little Bear played bear-run-about-by-himself

and Big Bear closed his

eyes for a think.

Little Bear went to
speak to Big Bear,
but Big Bear was …

asleep!

"Wake up, Big Bear!" Little Bear said.

Big Bear opened his eyes.

"I've played all my games

by myself," Little Bear said.

Big Bear thought for a bit, then he said,

"Let's play hide-and-seek, Little Bear."

"I'll hide and you seek," Little Bear said,

and he ran off to hide.

"I'm coming now!" Big Bear called,

and he looked till he

found Little Bear.

Then Big Bear hid, and Little Bear looked.

"I found you, Big Bear!" Little Bear said.

"Now I'll hide again."

They played lots of bear-games.

When the sun slipped away through

the trees, they were still playing.

Then Little Bear said,

"Let's go home now, Big Bear."

Big Bear and Little Bear went
home to their cave.
"We've been busy today, Little Bear!"
said Big Bear.
"It was lovely, Big Bear," Little Bear
said. "Just you and me playing …

together."